OLD LONDON

THE UNWANTED

(*Edwardian*)

OLD LONDON

THE UNWANTED

(*Edwardian*)

By
E. F. BENSON

Decorations by Reginald Birch

D. APPLETON-CENTURY COMPANY
INCORPORATED

NEW YORK　　　1937　　　LONDON

THE UNWANTED

THE UNWANTED

I

MISS DOROTHY VINCENT put her Pekinese dog on a lead, and, stepping briskly across the road from her aunt's house, let herself and Chang (known also as "Strong Mannie") into the garden of Beaconsfield Square, where she gave him his liberty. That was always the first duty of the day as soon as she was dressed: rain or sun or frost or snow she took Chang for his early constitutional. He was *too* intelligent about snow: he had found out, the very first time he saw it, that though it looked solid, it was something to drink. How wonderful dogs were! On this warm windless April morning it was quite unnecessary for her to wear hat or cloak, but Strong Mannie had not been very well this last day or two, and she strapped round him his blanket coat embroidered with his initials.

"Mummie knows best, dear," she whispered, and wagged his plumed tail for him, to Chang's great disgust, in order to show that he was pleased.

Dorothy did everything briskly. She was a short, energetic woman of middle age, of full figure and of eager countenance. Wherever she was and whatever she was doing, she distilled from the trivial round a constant flow of interest and excitement, which she served up to her friends hot and foaming, like the lightest of soufflés, with the added sauce of her own appreciation poured over it. Just now she was intent on making Chang enjoy himself. ("We don't *deserve* to have dogs," she often said, "unless we make them happy. They're so absolutely dependent on us and so devoted, aren't they? I always think a dog's devotion is one of the most beautiful things in the world.") She hid

herself behind the rustic summer-house on
the lawn, in order to make Chang think she
was lost and be filled with joyful rapture at
finding her again, which he was sure to do at
once, because he was so clever, and his joy
would more than make up for his anxiety.
But just now Chang was absorbed in pursu-
ing some interesting smell across the grass
which seemed to promise a lady at the end
of it, and it was a matter of total indiffer-
ence to him whether his mistress was lost for
evermore. He followed the scent round the
summer-house and did not take the smallest
notice of Dorothy when he discovered her.
She threw a stick for Chang, but he let it lie
there unheeded, and finally she ran down the
garden-path for Chang (such a swift Strong
Mannie!) to chase her. That took his fancy,
especially since the interesting smell led to
the locked garden-gate and could be pursued
no farther; he galloped after her in his grotesque Chinese mode, and they had a lovely
race round a flower-bed till Dorothy was out

of breath and allowed herself to be caught.

"Of course dogs have souls," she thought. "I should lose all my faith in a future life if I wasn't sure that they were going to share it with us."

The bed round which this hunt had careered was planted with daffodils now in full flower. Dorothy gazed at them enraptured and tried to remember that lovely poem which Wordsworth (or was it Keats?) had written about them. "I know it ends 'And dances with the daffodils,' " she said to herself. "And there's another by Herrick, and isn't there something by Shakespeare? I must look them up and read them to Auntie Alice. Poor dear, how snappy she was last night, but who wouldn't be with that horrid rheumatism? So brave about it usually. How I admire bravery! I must see if I can't keep her mind off herself today. That's the secret of being happy. If she only could think about others, she would have no time for thinking about herself.... Chang, don't run after that cat. Naughty!"

Dorothy had come to the lower end of the oblong (inaccurately known as the Square) and the traffic was roaring by up and down the street. Girls and boys and women and men were waiting at the corner where the omnibuses stopped and swarmed up the stairs. The sight of the busy crowd always filled her with profound speculations. It was so thrilling to reflect that they all had lives of their own to live and work of their own to do. Some carried despatch-cases and paper packages, and Dorothy, holding Chang in her arms, suggested to him that they contained their lunch: did Chang think they had some nice bones? One young man was clasping his arm round a girl's waist: Chang agreed with her that they were engaged or perhaps married. But she had to tear herself away from this intriguing spectacle, for Strong Mannie had had his quarter of an hour's exercise, and she wanted her breakfast. How it freshened one up (and Chang, too) to get this breath of air first thing in the morning!

Auntie Alice, she knew, was staying in bed, and Dorothy had a sound meal by herself. She always told her friends that she never had any breakfast: just a cup of tea and one piece of toast, so her poached egg, her potted meat and her marmalade were a mere *hors d'œuvre*. There was a letter for her, which, the parlour-maid told her, had been sent up to her aunt by mistake. Mrs. Troubridge (with her apologies) had opened it before she saw to whom it was addressed, but Dorothy instantly reminded herself that Auntie Alice was far too honourable a woman to have read it. . . . The letter was from Evelyn, the wife of her brother Bernard. Bernard was abroad on some business of his firm's, and Dorothy had offered herself to spend a week with her sister-in-law at their charming house at the edge of the New Forest close to the coast.

Her two sons would be at home for their school holidays, and Dorothy had indicated very delicately to Evelyn that she knew she would not be up to doing much just now, and would have to take care of herself and lie down a good deal. So she thought she might be of use in "romping about" with Harry and Teddy, and in driving with Evelyn and reading to her. But Evelyn's reply proved to be far from enthusiastic. The boys, she said, would be having a couple of friends from Eton staying with them, and she herself had a sister to keep her company. She would, of course, be charmed to see Dorothy if she settled to come, but the house would be rather full, and if she decided to put off her visit for a few weeks, Bernard would be home again and would be sorry to have missed her. Certainly even the most optimistic could not consider this a warm welcome, and Dorothy felt rather chilled by it. A week in the New Forest in this resplendent month of spring would have been very pleasant, and she felt quite equal to romping about with four boys. She liked boys: they were so spontaneous.

She laid the letter down, uncertain whether to go or not. Poor Evelyn! How sincerely she pitied her! She had married Bernard when she was only seventeen, and now her sons were getting quite big fellows. Harry, the eldest, was eighteen, and the younger, Teddy, was as old as his mother was when she married: and after all these years there was another baby coming, like a postscript! Evelyn would soon be going through that terrible experience again, the bodily disfigurement, the sickness, the hours of travail, the peril, and, if all went well, the nursing of her baby. Dorothy had been in the house when Teddy was born, and the memory of it was repulsive and fascinating. The birth had been premature, midwife and doctor had been sent for hurriedly, and Evelyn had suffered dreadful hours. How useful she herself had been: the doctor told her so and thanked her warmly. She had kept Bernard occupied (poor Bernard, he somehow felt that it was his fault), she had taken him for walks, she had played chess with him, even though he could hardly attend at all. "Thank God," thought Dorothy, "I was always determined that I would never marry. Nothing would induce me to go through that. How can a woman face it?" Yet how enchanting a small baby was, and there seemed to be no other way of getting one.

Her last visit to her brother and Evelyn had been in the preceding August, and, while still pondering whether, in spite of this tepid welcome, she should go, she recalled these later memories, as she scooped up the spilt yolk of her poached egg, with singular minuteness.... The garden, with a couple of tennis lawns, was bordered by a broad belt of fir trees beyond which lay a sandy creek that filled and emptied with the tidal river. Harry and Teddy were there in their summer holidays, and she had had a lovely game

of tennis with them one morning: she was
so anxious to learn to play, and Harry, as
being the stronger, took her as partner. Such
an exciting game, thought Dorothy; they
nearly won, and when it was over she proposed a bathe in the creek before lunch.
Neither of the boys seemed keen about it,
and she chaffed them for their lack of energy,
till she remembered that growing boys often
felt tired. So she established herself in a
deck-chair with a volume of Pepys's Diary.
Sammy Pepys was such a droll companion,
and it was only right to overlook the coarse-
ness of the age he lived in. He had the same
busy gusto for life that she had: what talks
they would have had together about sermons
and food and theatres and housemaids. She
read for an hour, and then strolled down
across the lawn to the belt of fir trees. The
water of the creek, now at full tide, gleamed
like wedges of silver between the tawny-red
trunks, and she wished she had brought her
paint-box to make a sketch. But it was a

lovely morning for a bathe: there was a cabin on the foreshore and she knew she had a costume there. Though it was dull bathing alone —Harry was teaching her to swim, and said she would soon be quite a fish—a dip before lunch would be very pleasant. She would practise industriously, though Harry was not there to support with a hand beneath her middle, and he would be surprised to see, when next they all bathed together, how she had got on: he would be proud of his pupil. She struck straight through the wood towards the creek, her steps silent on the muted floor of fir-needles.

She heard the sound of talk and laughter from somewhere close in front of her. She paused, then crept forward again concealing herself behind the trunks of the firs till she was close to the edge of the bank. There on the beach below were the two boys without a rag of clothing between them. They had evidently had a dip already, for their bodies gleamed with the wet film of water, and now they were lying a-bask in the sun, arguing about something. Then they both jumped up: Teddy, shorter by two inches than his brother, grasped him round the neck with one arm and crooked the other between Harry's elbow and his body. It must be some wrestling hold—they had talked about the Japanese jiu-jitsu at breakfast—that they were trying. Dorothy gasped with pleasure, her blood beat quick with a sudden joy: they were like a lovely group of Greek statuary come to life. Then Teddy flung forward his leg between Harry's knees, and next moment he had swung him off his feet and laid him flat on the sand.

Dorothy completely forgot herself.

"Oh, well done, Teddy," she cried. "That was neat!"

She recollected herself, and, suffused with blushes, she crept away back to the lawn, and resumed, with less absorption, her reading of Pepys's Diary. Surely they could not have seen her, and probably they had not heard her irresponsible exclamation for they were both so taken up with their wrestling. But how queer of them to have slipped off to have a bathe alone, when, just now, they had shewn so little inclination for it.

Half an hour afterwards they came strolling together towards the house. Dorothy, buried in her book, remained unaware of their approach till they were close to her. She was, of course, going to be quite ignorant that they had been bathing at all.

Harry's voice caused her to look up.

"What a studious P.W.," he said, and he and Teddy burst out laughing.

That was an old family joke: Dorothy arranged her abundant auburn hair in the fashion of the Princess of Wales. A little odd that they should have both laughed so much, for the nickname was commonly used without making merriment.

"Her Royal Highness is enjoying her study, too," she said eagerly. "Have either of you read the Diary of my beloved Samuel

Pepys? I've been devouring his account of the great fire of London. Too thrilling. They blew up quantities of houses to isolate it, but it still advanced till it reached the end of the street where Pepys lived, and he dug a hole in his garden and buried his money there and his Parmesan cheese. Then, wasn't it lucky? they got the fire under, and Sammy lost nothing. You don't mean to tell me it's lunch-time, do you? How the morning has flown!"

There was a rather disconcerting sequel: or was it only her imagination, Dorothy asked herself, as she finished her marmalade. ... They played a favourite game of hers after dinner that evening, at which she was very nimble. A mixed lot of letters of the alphabet on small cardboard squares were laid face downwards on the table: two of them were turned over, and whoever first said some name or well-known phrase of which they were the initial letters appropriated them. The player who had got most

letters in his store at the end was the winner.
Dorothy was rapidly accumulating them:
she had said "God forbid" for G.F., "Boil-
ing Point" for B.P., "Signs of the Zodiac"
for the difficult S.Z., and had been far too
quick for the others. But when P.W. had
turned up, she had not time to say the obvious "Princess of Wales" before Teddy
shouted "Potiphar's Wife": and Evelyn as
well as the two boys had burst out laughing.

"Well done, Teddy!" said Dorothy en-
couragingly. "Somewhere in Genesis, isn't
she? That's what comes of getting a prize
for divinity at Eton."

She could not accurately remember what
Potiphar's wife had done, and with her usual
thirst for interesting information, she turned
over the pages of her Bible when she went to
bed, and found out. What foul-minded boys
they were! Evidently they had seen her when
they were wrestling this morning and told
their mother. Besides, Potiphar's wife had
done something quite different.

But they had all been very nice to her afterwards. They had bathed together in those ample and discreet garments which were correct for mixed bathing: a two-piece suit for Dorothy, a tunic of serge with sleeves coming down to the elbow and loose trousers tied round the ankles: for the boys a one-piece suit buttoning up to the neck and covering arms and legs to elbows and knees. Harry gave her a swimming-lesson supporting her with a hand below her bosom as she kicked out her short plump legs. Then Teddy tried to teach her to serve overhand at tennis. Very hot work it was and Dorothy said she was too tired to go on when she saw how transparent her blouse was becoming. They drove to a ruined Abbey, and she explained to them how Norman architecture passed into Early English, and how lancet windows enlarged when tracery was invented. No longer were they foul-minded animals: Dorothy buried Potiphar's wife (if they meant any personal application) and never thought of her again till she received this morning that unwelcoming letter from Evelyn.

It was plain that Evelyn did not want her, and instantly she became a very unfriendly sort of woman, the sort of woman you had to be cautious about. That was the way Dorothy's mind worked. If a friend gave a party and did not ask her, she went quite out of favour, and Dorothy did not scruple to say unkind things about her: she was horrid to her servants, or she was looking terribly old, or it was unwise to trust her with a secret. But if that friend subsequently asked her to spend a week-end, or gave her a nice birthday present, she was reinstated at once and became the cleverest and wittiest and most marvellous of people. . . . So now Evelyn was outcast: she was a vulgar woman who enjoyed coarse jokes, and Dorothy decided not to pay the visit she had herself proposed. She must somehow account to Auntie Alice for this change of plans without letting her know that Evelyn did not want her, for in her bright picture of herself on which she loved to dwell, her friends were always clamouring for her presence and gave her no peace till they got her. Deep in thought over this point, she finished her toast and marmalade, and went upstairs to see how Auntie Alice was and to cheer her up. She took the morning paper with her, which she had had no time to look at, in order to read the news to her.

Odd sounds of notes of the piano being struck singly or in octaves came from the drawing-room, and Dorothy remembered that the tuner was here this morning. She would like to see how he worked: it was so wonderful to be able to tune pianos: one ought to know about it. She slipped quietly in and saw a young man sitting there wearing large dark spectacles.

"Good morning," she said, "I shan't disturb you, I hope, if I listen for a few minutes, for I've always wanted to know how pianos are tuned. So clever of you: just by ear, is it? Do you strike each note again and again till it sounds quite right with its octave? And do tell me: what's that sort of gimlet—no, I see it's a key—which you fit on to those pegs? Why do you do that?"

"To tighten the strings up, if the note has gone flat, ma'am," he said. "The same way in which you tune up a violin."

"Really! The same as in tuning a violin! I never knew that!" said Dorothy. "How ignorant one is! And I suppose that if the note has gone sharp, you let it down. What an ingenious idea! Who invented it?"

"I couldn't say, ma'am."

Dorothy noticed that his spectacles were so dark that nothing of his eyes could be seen through them.

"I hope you haven't any trouble with your eyes," she said.

"Yes, ma'am, I'm blind."

"Oh, I do sympathise with you!" cried Dorothy. "What a dreadful misfortune!

How did it happen? Did it come on gradually?"

"Born like that, ma'am."

"How terrible for you! I wonder why such cruel things happen, don't you? So you've never even seen a piano, and do it all by ear. I suppose you can read Braille quite easily. What a wonderful invention, isn't it? I went to see an institution for blind children once, and they were all so brave. Quite cheerful, and walking about as if nothing was the matter. The matron told me they develop some special sense of touch. Isn't that wonderful? Have you got it, too? I'm sure you must have, for I noticed at once, when I was coming upstairs, what a wonderful touch you had."

He waited till she had finished, and then struck the octave again.

"That sounds absolutely right," said Dorothy. "And now do you go on to the next? All the way up the piano to the very top? Those top notes, and I suppose the bottom ones, must be the hardest to get right, aren't they?"

"Yes, ma'am. But if you'll excuse me, I must go on with my work, which I can't if there's talking. I've got several other pianos to tune this morning, and I'm a little behind-hand already."

"Oh, I'm so glad you've got plenty of work," she said. "It is so sad when people who want to work can't find any, isn't it? And I must go to see my Aunt, who's got rheumatism. I'm so much interested in all you've told me, and thank you so much for tuning the piano for me. It is a good piano, isn't it? And it will be a pleasure to play on it again, especially since you've told me how it is tuned. Damp weather affects pianos, or isn't that true? I hope you will find your way downstairs all right."

She gathered up the paper and went quickly upstairs to her aunt's room.

"Dear Auntie Alice, I'm a little late," she said, "but I had to say a few words to the piano-tuner. Just fancy: he's blind: is it not terrible for him? But I think I made him feel how truly I sympathised with him, and he was so calm; not a word of complaint. One can do so much for people by sympathy, don't you think? And how are you this morning?"

"Not a very good night," said Aunt Alice.

"I am so sorry. A bad night is fatiguing, isn't it, instead of being refreshing. But you're so wonderful: you always make light of that sort of thing, which would make me so grumpy. I had such a charming letter from Evelyn—the one sent up to you by mistake—and she was ever so pleased that I thought I might be able to come to stay with her next week."

"That's all right then, Dolly," said Aunt Alice very cordially. "It will do you a world of good to get a week in the country, and Evelyn and the boys will be so pleased to see you—"

"We'll talk about that presently," said

Dorothy. "I haven't looked at the paper yet: I thought I would keep it to read to you. The South African War? Not much news from there. How terrible it is to think that there are so many people who want to kill each other; don't you think so, Auntie Alice? How can they say their prayers at night, and then go out to shoot each other next morning? It all seems to me so sad, and very likely they would be great friends if they weren't enemies. And Lord Roberts: everyone says he's so kind and such a true Christian, and yet he plans these dreadful slaughters. I suppose he has to, as he's Commander-in-Chief, but it must be awful for him. I often think that there's something wrong with the world, don't you, when so many people kill each other on purpose. Then the Queen has gone to Ireland. Isn't that gallant of her at her age? Wouldn't it be wonderful to be the Queen and to be able to do so much for your country? That must sustain her. I'm sure if you were Queen, Auntie Alice, you would work yourself to death for your country, in spite of your rheumatism, and she's got it, too, hasn't she? It is such a great position, don't you think, and so responsible."

"Yes, dear, very great, very responsible," said Aunt Alice, lifting herself in bed in order to shift the position of the rheumatic leg.

Instantly Dorothy sprang to her feet.

"Wait till I help you," she said. "Now lean on my shoulder as heavily as you like, and that will support you. Don't be afraid to put your weight on it: I'm so strong."

"No: I can manage much better for myself, thank you," said Aunt Alice. "Take your shoulder away, dear, and let me get hold of the bed-post. There! And is there nothing in the paper about that interesting murder? Surely the trial must have been going on all yesterday."

"Yes, nearly a whole page," said Dorothy glancing rapidly at the summary. It looked very exciting: a crime of passion, a youthful husband, a nagging elderly wife, a mistress, the wife's body cut in pieces and buried in the garden with a yew hedge planted above it.... But it was contrary to her avowed principles to take any interest in such ugly things as infidelity and murder and adultery. So dangerous to admit such poison-germs into the mind; you couldn't tell how they might spread.

"It all looks too horrid, dear Auntie," she said. "I don't think I could read it aloud to you. Now about my staying with darling Evelyn. I hate disappointing her, and it's so sweet of you to want me to have a week of springtime in the country—*Primavera,* what a lovely word, isn't it? It reeks of flowers—but that's so like you. I always say you are the most unselfish woman I know. But I won't go: that's that, as the servants say. I'm going to stop here till you're quite yourself again."

"No need whatever, Dolly," said Aunt Alice with emphasis. "I shall be quite comfortable and happy alone. Rest, for body and mind alike, is the important thing; the quieter I keep the better. That's what Dr. Dobbie told me yesterday. With Bernard away, you would be the greatest comfort to Evelyn, and, as you say, she would be most disappointed if you didn't go."

"Dear Auntie, impossible," said Dorothy. "I can be ever so obstinate if I'm driven into a corner. Besides I shouldn't have a moment's peace if I went. Put it like that! Put it that I'm only selfishly thinking of my own comfort. I should always be fearing to receive news from Jacobs that you weren't getting stronger, or that you seemed very depressed with nobody to cheer you up and chat with you and read to you. I shall telegraph to Evelyn to say that I'm unavoidably prevented from coming. Letter follows. I shall write that very carefully—it's so cruel, isn't it, to alarm people when there's no immediate need—and say that you aren't very well, and that I don't like to leave you, though there's no cause for anxiety. Now I must go out to do my jobs. How they accumulate, don't they? I'll come up and see you again as soon as I get in."

Dorothy picked up the morning paper: she wanted to read about the murder trial.

"You might leave it with me, dear," said Aunt Alice. "I should like to glance at it. And never mind about coming up to see me again before lunch. Very likely I shall be having a nap after my broken night."

Dorothy kissed her. Auntie certainly looked tired.

She thought she had managed that business pretty well, and that there was no doubt in the invalid's mind that she was giving up her week in the country for her sake. Yet you never could be sure about Auntie Alice. Dorothy could well remember a rather painful occasion when some friend had neglected her, and in consequence she had told her aunt that everybody tried to avoid playing tennis with this miscreant because she cheated, declaring that services she could not take were faults. Aunt Alice had looked at her very steadily while she embroidered this indictment and at the end said, "Now, Dolly, that's not true!" Very disconcerting....

There was a full morning before her. First she went down to the kitchen to hold a catering conference with Cooper, whom she always addressed playfully as "Mrs. Cook." Auntie Alice usually saw to the commissariat, but, now that she was incapacitated, Dorothy felt it her duty to go into everything very thoroughly; else there was sure to be waste. She looked into the meat-safe and found quite a large piece of cold mutton there: that was for the servants' dinner, Mrs. Cook explained: slices cut off and grilled. That sounded delicious, and Dorothy asked to have a slice sent up for her lunch. That and some bread and cheese was all she would need. Or perhaps some stewed prunes. So wholesome.

"And then there's Mrs. Troubridge's dinner, Mrs. Cook," she said. "She looks so pulled down: we must tempt her appetite. How about a little cold soup first: I know how delicious your cold soup is, and a grilled cutlet and then some jelly, so light and digestible, isn't it? Oh, I've got such a good idea! Instead of the cutlet let us give her a roast partridge, cut in half: the other half would do for my dinner, or you might keep it to give to Auntie Alice cold for her lunch tomorrow. She'll like to have her dinner early, I expect, and then I can go and talk to her before she settles down for the night. And you mustn't worry about me at all. There'll be so much extra work with carrying meals upstairs. Jacobs can give me my half-partridge, if we settle it that way, and I'll have some simple pudding and a hot savoury brought in when I ring, and she can bring my coffee along with that, and put it down in the fender, for I think I'll have a fire in the dining-room this evening, as it

gets chilly after sunset in April, however
warm the day may have been. So that's all
settled, isn't it, Mrs. Cook? How quickly two
people can get through their business, if they
put their heads together!"

Mrs. Cook had not yet been able to get a
word in.

"You won't be able to get a partridge,
miss, in April," she observed. "At least I
don't know where. And Mrs. Troubridge has
already written out the meals for the day."

"Oh, Mrs. Cook, why didn't you tell me
that?" cried Dorothy. "How naughty of you
to have wasted our time like this! Then you
don't want me to do any shopping for you?"

"No, miss, thank you," said Cooper. "I'll
be going out to do my marketing presently."

So that duty could be dismissed, though
with a momentary suspicion that Mrs. Cook
had received no orders at all, and intended
to get something specially delicious for
downstairs. Then she must buy some flowers
for Auntie Alice's room: flowers looked so

fresh and cheerful by a bed-side: they diverted the invalid's thoughts from herself to springtime and sunshine. She must change the library books, and she hurried upstairs again to find if there was any particular book her aunt wanted. Auntie was deep in the murder trial, but rose to the surface to say she had not nearly finished the book she was reading: then submerged herself again.

"It was lucky I came up to ask!" said Dorothy. "How well I should have deserved my scolding if I had returned it without asking you! And, oh, how stupid I've been. I told Mrs. Cook to get a nice young partridge for your dinner, forgetting that it was April! Such a snub I got from the dear woman! Quite comfortable, Auntie Alice, or as comfortable as possible?"

"Quite!" said Aunt Alice....

So there was no need to go to the Library: she regretted that, for there was a most intelligent man there: so well-read, and if he recommended a book it was sure to be an interesting one: her taste and his were wonderfully similar. Perhaps she could find time just to drop in and talk over what Auntie Alice would be likely to want next. And a note from the Vicar had arrived while she was upstairs, asking if she would help in decorating the church for Easter. Of course she would. Such a truly apostolic man, and so good to the poor. Dorothy sometimes asked him about the slums and overcrowding in the parish, and the dreadful evils that resulted from it. A whole family, with grown up sons and daughters sleeping in one room, she had heard. She had thought of getting him to take her to one of the worst houses that she might see for herself what the conditions were, but the fear of bringing back the germs of some dreadful disease and of Auntie Alice catching it deterred her from doing anything so dangerous. But Easter decorations by all means: she would pop into the Vicarage and say that it would be a joy. Then there was the telegram and the letter (that had better be written at once) to Evelyn, explaining that Auntie Alice was not at all well, and, though there was nothing to be anxious about, she did not like to leave her. There was no difficulty about the composition of this: Auntie Alice, she wrote, who never thought of herself, urged her to go, but she looked so sad at the idea of her departure, that Dorothy knew what she really felt about it. And she looked so happy when Dorothy said she would put her visit off, that she was sure she had decided right.

Finally she must pay an urgent errand of comfort and helpfulness to her friend Sylvia Atchison. She had heard several little stories lately which made her fear that Sylvia and her husband were not as happy together as they should be. They had dined together at the Carlton, and had talked in very loud voices as if they were quarrelling: they had been to a dance and Toby had left her to come home alone: Sylvia had spent last week-end in London while he had entertained

some men-friends at their house in the country. Dorothy felt that, if these stories were
true, there was an opportunity for a devoted
friend to be very useful, for Sylvia would
find it a great relief to confide in an older
woman who was so anxious to help. Both
she and Toby were young and strong-willed
and wanted their own way, and though
Dorothy had not personally experienced the
frictions of the married, she knew what it
was to live with Aunt Alice, and the need
of constant tact, and the duty of self-sur-
render. That visit might be a long one, for
Sylvia would want to pour out the whole of
her difficulties and grievances, and it was
high time for Dorothy to set out, for between sympathising with the piano-tuner
and cheering up Aunt Alice and consulting
Mrs. Cook (how servants appreciated a little
friendly familiarity: it made them feel that
they were members of the family instead of
merely serving it!) and writing to Evelyn,
it was already eleven o'clock.

II

She started up the Square towards the Vicarage in order to tell the Vicar how pleased she would be to help with the Easter decorations. If he was in, he would be sure to want her to sit down and have a few minutes' chat, but she would not be able to stop long. He got little chance of a quiet talk at home; for his sister, with whom he lived, was not much of a companion to him. She was terribly deaf, poor thing—such an affliction: almost as distressing as being like the piano-tuner—and it was very tiring for him to shout at her. Such intercourse must be very fatiguing instead of refreshing. And Virginia was no use in the parish: of course her deafness made it impossible for her to go district visiting, for who could bawl out domestic and intimate worries? He ought really to marry: a clergyman ought to be married, whatever the Roman Catholics said, for an energetic and truly Christian wife—

and, oh, how lucky that Dorothy had not been a minute later, for there they both were, just coming out of the Vicarage. It stood at the top of the long Square, and though she waved to them, she felt sure that they could not have seen her, for they turned to walk quickly down the far side of the Square with the garden intervening between them and her. Luckily again—she was in luck this morning—she had not gone far, and could easily turn back round the bottom of the Square and meet them when they emerged at the corner where the buses stopped. This manœuvre was most successful: she was in plenty of time, and concealing herself behind the garden-railings she watched them getting nearer and nearer and when they were quite close, she jumped playfully out on them.

Dorothy raised her voice to the requisite pitch. Deaf people, she knew, often suffered from strange unhappy suspicions, if they could not hear what was said, that they were

being talked about, and she would be very
sorry if Virginia thought that.

"Good morning, Miss Virginia," she
shouted. "Good morning, dear Reverence.
What a celestial morning, and, oh! the dancing daffodils in the garden! Strong Mannie
and I could hardly help dancing, too! I was
just coming to tell you how delighted I shall
be to help with the Easter decorations.
Please, may I deck the pulpit? I shall make
a positive bower for you, so that you feel
you *must* preach about the lilies of the field
and Solomon in all his glory. Arums, probably, weren't they? Easter is always such a
joyful festival, don't you think, Reverence,
though you shall never persuade me that it
oughtn't to be fixed like Christmas. Something about the Paschal Moon, isn't it, just
as if we were Jews. I can't believe we're the
lost tribes, can you, Miss Virginia. I don't
feel like a lost tribe, so what have we to do
with the Jewish passover? So much better
to have it fixed, and then we should know

where we are without hunting about in the Calendar."

The knot of people waiting at the corner where the buses stopped stood open-mouthed with wonder at this loud monologue. During it Miss Virginia made a sign to a passing cab-driver, and before it was over a four-wheeler had drawn up at the kerb. She touched her brother on the shoulder and stepped into it without a word.

"Thank you so much, Miss Dorothy," he said, dodging round her across the pavement. "By all means do the pulpit: most good of you. And we must have a talk about the Paschal Moon sometime, for there's a great deal to be said on both sides, but just now I see Virginia's waiting for me."

Dorothy knew how much he enjoyed a talk with her, and it was vexing to have their chat cut short by Virginia's hailing a cab in that abrupt manner. But a fairly satisfactory reason occurred to her.

"Of course, he had to go," she said to herself, "when she scurried into the cab, though I could see that he didn't want to. And I've noticed before that she will never leave us in peace if we're having a talk. Poor thing! What needless anxieties people make for themselves, as if the idea of marrying him ever occurred to me. But it all hangs together, and it's that she's afraid of. What a grim surly watch-dog, and what a perfect name Virginia is for her! The very archetype of the jealous withered spinster!"

She gave a shrill exclamation and dismissed Virginia from her mind. A young man got out of the bus which had stopped close beside her. He wheeled round at once to cross the road, but her sharp eyes had caught a glimpse of his face.

"Harry!" she cried, but he could not have heard her, and she ran after him.

"Dear blind bat!" she said. "It's Dolly. You in London, and I heard from your darling Mummie only this morning, and she said nothing about your coming up. Oh, let us get on to the pavement at once: that rude hansom-driver nearly ran over me, and then we can talk. How lovely to see you! Account for yourself, truant boy. Such luck to have run across you like this. If I had been a second later, or you a second sooner, we should have missed each other."

"Mother didn't know I was coming, when she wrote to you," said Harry. "I came up quite suddenly on the spur of the moment. I—"

"Harry, I must interrupt you," said Dorothy, "or I shall forget. Have you heard the new riddle: Why did the man get up so quick? Can't you guess?"

"No," said he.

"Because he had sat down on the spur of the moment. Rather naughty, but heavenly, don't you think?"

"Ripping," said Harry. "As to accounting for myself, I'm going off to the Riviera where I shall meet father—"

"How delightful for you. Give him my love."

"—and I wanted to book a berth on the Blue train. And then I had toothache last night, so it was well to see my dentist. I'm going there now: I'm rather late."

"Then come and have lunch with me afterwards," said Dorothy. "See your dentist and take your tickets; there'll be heaps of time. Poor dear, I hope he won't hurt you, but, just in case, I'll tell Mrs. Cook to give us something soft, mince and a pudding you needn't bite: no trouble at all. Auntie Alice would love to see you, but I doubt if she's up to it, so I shan't tell her you're here. She's in bed, poor dear, so rheumatic—how I wish I could bear it for her—and rather in the dumps: she didn't seem to care about seeing anyone this morning, and her doctor told her to keep very quiet. That's all settled then. Lovely to see you at half-past one. Just you and the Princess of Wales."

Dorothy was pleased with herself for hav-

ing said the "Princess of Wales." It would
imply that she had quite forgotten about the
sinister lady in Genesis with the same initials
and all that horrid incident. Then a distressing but interesting doubt occurred to her.
Surely Evelyn had said in her letter—how
lucky that she had kept it—that Harry and
Teddy would be having friends staying with
them next week which would make the house
very full and there was Harry telling her
that he was taking tickets by the Blue train
for the Riviera. One of them must be telling
fibs, and she remembered how often it had
struck her that Evelyn was not really to be
trusted. Hitherto that had only been a suspicion, but now it was confirmed. Evelyn had
not wanted her visit, and had made up that
rubbish about the boys having friends with
them. It would be awkward for her when
Harry told her about this encounter and she
recalled what she had said in her letter. Or
was Harry deceiving her? She had thought
for a moment that he had tried to avoid her.

Was he really up in London on some other errand, to spend the day perhaps with some dreadful woman who was making love to him? The Blue train and the dentist might only be some invention, and Dorothy congratulated herself on being so quick with him, and pinning him down to lunch with her before he could think of any excuse. The best train back to his home she knew was at 3.40: it might be well to go to the station with him and see him off. Young men were so easily entrapped by designing women, and this meeting was providential, if there was anything of that sort on foot. How handsome he was, and his well-fitting clothes did not conceal the strength of his square shoulders and the lithe grace of his long limbs, and how swiftly, as if by the stroke of a scythe, had Teddy swept him off his feet and laid him on the sand.

Dorothy recalled herself to her other jobs. What a blessing it was, she reflected, that she had so much to do for others, and had no room for anything in her mind except her service to them: Harry, Aunt Alice and Sylvia, all so dear, and all needing her so, were enough to keep even her busy. She had better go to Sylvia next, and try to put things right there, and then on her way home she could buy the flowers for Auntie Alice, and pop down to the kitchen to see Mrs. Cook about soft food for Harry.... She looked forward eagerly to her interview with Sylvia, for there was the prospect of being a true, helpful friend to her. She knew Sylvia's faults: she was quick of temper and sharp of tongue, and very obstinate. As for that touch of vanity, who would not be vain with such a lovely face? It was foolish, thought Dorothy, to minimise a friend's faults: if you are to be of use, you have to recognise them and wrestle with them. And there was so much that was fine in Sylvia: she had a warm heart and generous impulses if you could succeed in arousing them. There was something deliciously child-like about her, too: a puckish sense of humour: she was given to practical jokes, such as putting a cushion on your chair, which, when you sat down on it, emitted a wild yowling noise, as if you had sat down on the cat, and then Sylvia screamed with laughter. Of late the two had not seen much of each other, for Dorothy had reason to suspect that Sylvia had given a musical party a month or so ago, to which she had not been bidden. Dorothy had purposely not told her that she was coming this morning to try to make her take a truer view of matrimony and its delicate obligations, its give and take: if you descended on people suddenly, in a billow of affection and helpfulness, you often swept them off their feet (as Teddy had done to Harry) whereas if they knew you were coming and why, they were apt to entrench themselves behind a wall of defensive pride.

Sylvia was in and would see her. She lived in a beautiful house, overlooking the Park, full of lovely things, but how pathetically hollow were these treasures of art if happiness was wanting! Dorothy particularly noticed a jade bowl on the hall-table, which she was sure she had not seen before, and, as Sylvia knew, she adored jade. She had two or three pieces of her own, but clumsy stuff compared with this bowl, delicately thin and transparent, and exquisitely carved. She lingered a moment, looking at it, and then the footman took her up in the lift to the third floor where was Sylvia's sitting-room. He was a handsome young man: Sylvia had always good-looking servants, but she never managed to keep them long. Interested in everything, she asked the man how the lift worked. It was so cleverly contrived that if you wanted to go to the third floor, you only had to shut the door of the lift and press the third button. There was time for several eager questions: What happened if you didn't shut the door of the lift? How did the lift *know* which the third floor was? How did it ever get back to the ground floor, when you had left it up in the air? It was almost like a live thing, wasn't it?

Sylvia rose as she entered. She was very tall, and bent low to kiss her. Dorothy thought she looked worn and troubled and she must be both bright and tender with her.

"My dear, how lovely to see you," she said. "What an age since we met! And what a frock! A dream. I wish I could have such dreams! How wise you were to have your sitting-room high up. That marvellous view over the Park. All the trees bursting into leaf: it's like being in the heart of the country. I hoped I was going into the country next week to stay with Evelyn, you know Evelyn, I think. My dear, another baby coming after seventeen years. Almost a miracle: I didn't know such things could happen, did you? Bernard's abroad, and I thought I might be a companion to Evelyn. But she says the house will be full of the boys' friends, though I did meet one of my nephews just now, who says he's going to the Riviera. All rather muddled and confusing, and Auntie Alice far from well and very depressed and I don't like to leave her, so I must stop in London. How is your beloved Toby?"

Sylvia, as usual, tried in vain to keep pace with these topics and interrogations, and gave it up. She waited for the last and answered that.

"Rude health," she said. "Going abroad for Easter."

"You lucky people! Where are you going?"

"I'm not going with him," said Sylvia. "I shall stay with my mother while he's away."

This seemed to settle the matter in Dorothy's mind. It confirmed all she had heard: there certainly was trouble. The billow of affection and helpfulness collected itself and foamed forth.

"Dearest Sylvia, you and Toby have been very much on my mind lately," she said.

"I've been feeling instinctively—it's a sort of gift I have and I take no credit for it— that everything was not going very sweetly and joyfully with you. You know me so well, and how I never poke my nose into other people's affairs. But there's always been such a bond of sympathy between us, that I should never forgive myself if I didn't help you in any way I can, and I know you would do the same for me, wouldn't you? Loyalty and service to friends come before everything else, don't they?"

Sylvia made one fruitless attempt to get her head above the surge.

"But what are you talking about?" she said. "Toby and me, do you mean?"

The billow rushed on. It had become more like an avalanche, growing in speed and strength as it moved, and gathering into itself all kinds of miscellaneous débris.

"You're both so young, darling," said Dorothy, "and youth is apt to be impatient. I was impatient myself at your age, and, oh, how bitterly I've regretted it since. One so easily comes out with a hasty and wounding word, and a word once spoken—I forget who said it, but it's so true—can never be recalled, can it? Then there's the temptation, which I have known too, but always resist, to attribute a bad motive to something that may be meant quite amiably, don't you think? and worst of all unspoken suspicions that one cherishes instead of suppressing. Suspicion poisons all happiness, and distorts all we look on like a convex mirror or the mote and the beam in the parable. How wonderful the parables are, aren't they? And quarrels start from such small beginnings so easy to nip in the bud, but if they're allowed to grow they smother us."

Dorothy paused for one half-second to take breath, but Sylvia made no attempt to get out of the avalanche. On it poured again.

"So tell me all about it, darling. Confide in me for I've had so much experience in dealing with people who are not always very sweet-tempered—I don't know if you've ever seen Auntie Alice in one of her silent resentful moods, have you, when she carps at everything you do or say. And two people, though they love each other, can say or do things which they bitterly regret afterwards, and they can't bring themselves to apologise which would make everything all right again because their pride, though it's really nothing to be proud of, won't permit them. Those lovely lines of Tennyson, do you know them? about falling out with those we love and kissing again with tears. So true, though people decry Tennyson nowadays. But I'm sure something can be done, if you'll tell me all about it, and then I'll see Toby for you with pleasure. I always get on well with young men, almost *too* well, as Evelyn once said to me though, of course, that was only chaff. Dear me, I wonder if that's why she doesn't want me there next week, for she said there would be four boys in the house!

But never mind that. It's you and Toby I'm thinking about."

During the last section of this hurricane eloquence, Sylvia had left her chair, where she was directly faced with the gale of its outpouring, and was now standing with her back to Dorothy looking out of the window. Dorothy, who could pursue two trains of thoughts simultaneously with the utmost ease, was now convinced that some struggle was going on in her friend's mind. She was wrestling with her pride, she was trying to bring herself to confess that she had often been hasty and irritable with Toby, and was longing to open her heart to her. Dorothy hoped that she would be quick about it, for though it was sure to be very interesting, and must on no account be cut short, she had a lot of things to do. So simultaneously she made her plans. She could have her interview with Toby after she had seen Harry off at the station. Then she must take Chang for his walk in the Park—ah, she could bring

Chang here, and pop across the road afterwards. If all went well, as it was sure to do, and she brought Sylvia and Toby together again, she would offer to dine with them quietly this evening, for in the first glowing shyness of reconciliation, they would like to have her with them to chatter and carry on normally. It would be tactful to leave rather early, on the sound excuse of saying good night to Auntie Alice, and perhaps she would admire the jade bowl, as Sylvia and Toby, interlaced, came to the door to see her off, bless them.... And surely Sylvia's shoulders were shaking. She was suppressing her emotion so bravely, but it would be a great relief to her to have a good cry.

"It's all much worse than you can have any idea of, Dolly," said Sylvia in a low tremulous voice. "He—he hates me. I'm terrified of him. He bought a tin of weed-killer yesterday and a revolver—"

Dorothy gave a great gasp of horror, and sprang up.

"Sylvia! You don't say so!" she cried. "Oh, how thankful I am I spoke to you. You must leave him at once. You must give information to the police. You must telegraph to your mother—"

Sylvia turned round with stricken face and trembling lips. Then she suddenly collapsed with a screech of laughter into her chair. She laughed and she laughed.

"Oh dear, oh dear," she hiccoughed. "Dolly, you'll be the death of me some day. You funny meddlesome old thing, how can you be so absurd? You have such good intentions, but you are such an ass. Of course Toby and I have a scrap sometimes but we rather enjoy it. And kissing again with tears: you are a comic! And he's going abroad because he loves it, and I'm going to stay with my mother because I hate it. But do cure yourself of that awful habit of butting in and being helpful. It's so mischievous and some day you'll get yourself into a dreadful scrape. If I told Toby what you've been saying to me this morning, he would go off the deep end and tell me he would never have you in the house again. Luckily it amused me to hear you run on like that—I can't think how you do it—but it wouldn't amuse him, and you certainly wouldn't get the Easter present—oh, I oughtn't to have said that: forget it. But the idea of your thinking you could put things straight between me and Toby! You're too killing!"

The avalanche slowed down, spreading out into shining ripples.

"My dear, what a joy to know it's all a mistake," said Dorothy. "How wicked people are to hint such things, and I'm so glad I came, for now I know from your own lips that there's nothing in it. And I must fly: such a busy day, I don't know how I'll get through it, with Auntie Alice in bed, and Harry coming to lunch and the church decorations to think about, but how much better to wear oneself out for others than rust in laziness, don't you think? And—oh, I am such a baby—may I go down in the lift all alone and work it for myself? Your man was so clever in explaining it to me. *Au revoir,* darling. Your lovely frock!"

Further conversation, she felt, would have been difficult just then, and Dorothy hurried to the lift, and touched the wrong button and careered to the top of the house. That idiotic footman—he looked a half-wit —must have told her wrong. She thought she had better have another lesson before operating alone again, and she walked down the five flights of stairs to the ground floor, and let herself out. What a turn it had given her when Sylvia had spoken of the weed-killer and the revolver! That was the sort of brutality that Sylvia thought so amusing. And she had said brutal things, too, which had better be forgotten at once. Dorothy wondered what the Easter present would be. Was it possible—but she smothered that fond speculation, and observing a flower-seller with some plumes of mimosa in his basket, she darted across the street. They were rather expensive, but what a delicious smell! She carried them home and put them in water, and then remembering that Auntie Alice had said she did not want to be disturbed, as she might be having a nap before lunch, she took them down to the kitchen for Mrs. Cook to send up on the tray.

"And Mr. Harry is coming to have lunch with me," she said. "I met him quite by accident in the street, and, poor boy, he has had to go to the dentist this morning, half-mad with toothache, so in case it hurts him to bite we must devise something soft for him. Your beet-root *purée* is always so delicious, and then some mince, do you think? and a caramel pudding. Lovely!"

Dorothy had still half an hour to spare before Harry was due. She thought of playing the piano in order to see into what sweet harmony the blind man had brought it, but Auntie Alice might be snoozing (such an

odd time to choose for it!) and it would disturb her. Days sometimes went by without
Dorothy touching the piano at all: then suddenly she would feel it her duty to keep up
her playing (the parable of the talents) and
she practised scales and finger exercises for
an hour, and followed it up by fugues,
sonatas and nocturnes. "Dear Auntie," she
would say, "I hope it won't disturb you if
I practise a little with the soft pedal down.
I used to play rather well, so Papa said, and
you know how musical he was, and I don't
want to give it up altogether." If it was
summer Aunt Alice sat in the garden till
this carnival was over.

Dorothy worked off some deep-seated
restlessness during these bouts, some sense
of frustration. Her fingers were very nimble, and, as they sped over the keys, she
liked to imagine herself giving a recital at
St. James's Hall, or playing Beethoven's
"Emperor" with the orchestra. Today, in
spite of her strenuous morning, that prickly

restlessness possessed her, but, with Aunt
Alice having a nap (or more probably reading the murder trial), she must suffer its
unmitigated pangs. She must, as usual, sacrifice herself for others, and she went up to
her bedroom and arranged her hair in the
Alexandrine mode—such hair, an auburn
cascade reaching below her waist—and put
on a new blouse of emerald green silk and
a pair of very high-heeled shoes, for Harry
was so tall. The intoxicating breeze of
spring blew in through the open window, and
she felt herself to be like an Aeolian harp
hung in a verdant tree and vibrating in long
silver-toned notes to the stirrings of the
fruitful air. The Vicar and Virginia passed
along the pavement below, going home no
doubt to lunch. "Poor man," she thought,
"saddled with that dessicated spinster of a
sister: how much broader and fuller of
music his life ought to be!"

An itinerant barrel-organ with a monkey
in a scarlet jacket loitered into the Square,

and the young Italian grinder paid out Tosti's "Mattinata" with strident precision. Dorothy vibrated violently to that also, and fetched a couple of pennies from her store of coppers (so useful as tips for cab-drivers) and threw them down to him. Ought she to tell him to move on, lest he should disturb Auntie Alice's nap or her concentration on the murder trial, whichever happened to be occupying her? Altruism did not go as far as that: she was not responsible for the peregrinations of organ-grinders, and the exotic melody, the words of which she hummed to herself, woke some intimate echo in her heart. It paused for a moment as the performer picked up her largesse, and looked round to see where it had come from. He caught sight of her at her window, made a bow with a sweep of his hat and a smile of thanks on his merry face. She smiled in response, and denuded her store of two more pennies, and cried "Buon Giorno" to him: that would make the exile feel more at home.

Yet what a lovely life, she thought, to wander about the sunny streets in the exercise of his profession, distributing smiles and collecting pennies! How lovely, too, to be a good fairy to him like this, and, following an irresistible impulse, she ran downstairs: there was the monkey, too, she must be a good fairy to the monkey, poor starved little animal. Luckily there were some walnuts on the sideboard in the dining-room, and she took up a handful of these and went out into the street with them. Frustration again awaited her. The monkey looked at her, suspicious and melancholy, and did not want either her caresses or her nuts. The disagreeable creature: probably it was gorged with food already. She fared even worse with his master. Evidently he did not recognise her identity with the smiling girl who had already thrown four coppers to him from the upper window and cried "Buon Giorno" so sympathetically, for he held out his mendicant hat to her. Dorothy had no more pen-

nies, and, having no more Italian either, she
pointed to the window and then to herself
to establish the connection. But he did not
seem to understand, and she got only an ugly
scowl from him when she had nothing for
his hat, and he moved on up the Square. A
surly fellow, probably a burglar, and he had
got no business to be in the Square at all, for
there was a notice up on the garden-railings
that no street music (if you could call that
music) was allowed there. The proper thing
to do would be to call a policeman and get
him removed, but there was none in sight.

Dorothy went back into the house restless
and refrigerated. It was already a few minutes after half-past one, and Harry had not
yet arrived. She hated unpunctuality because it showed such thoughtlessness and
want of consideration for busy people to
keep them waiting just because you chose
to dawdle: all well-bred people were punc-
tual. And unpunctual people often made ex-
cuses for themselves so near falsehoods that

nobody could tell the difference. They said that they could not get a hansom or that their trains were late or their watches wrong. Dorothy was afraid that these habits were like twins, nurtured together; unpunctual people were usually untruthful. Evelyn was a sad instance of that: she was never in time for anything and really you could not trust what she said. That discrepancy for example (which must be looked into) between her assertion that her house next week would be full of boys, and Harry's assertion (Dorothy hoped soon to verify or disprove it) that he was taking tickets for the Blue train. Then came a ring at the front-door bell, and he was shown in.

"Lunch at once, Jacobs," she said in an audible aside to the parlour-maid by way of an oblique rebuke to him. "I began to be afraid that something had happened to you, dear. But I'm like that; if Chang doesn't lick his plate clean, I think he's ill. I suppose I shouldn't always be so full of anxious thoughts for others, but that's my nature, and I can't help it: I care too much, I expect. So delightful to see you, and I hope the dentist wasn't cruel, or cruel only to be kind. I believe they feel it terribly when they have to hurt their patients. And you got your tickets? Do let me see them. Those delicious little books of tickets in a green case with an elastic band. Yes: London to Dover: Dover to Calais: Calais to Paris: Ceinture railway: Gare de Lyons to Marseilles. Something so romantic about those little pages! Like magic carpets, aren't they, which will whirl you across Europe, while I toddle in the garden with Chang and give Auntie Alice her medicine."

Certainly the tickets were genuine: evidently then it was Evelyn who had been putting her off with false deterrents about the house being full of boys.

"What a lovely time you'll have, Harry," she said giving him back his magic carpet. "Just a few quiet days with your beloved mother first, and then Whizz! Ring the bell, will you? I can't think why lunch is so late."

"I don't know that they'll be very quiet days," said Harry. "A friend of mine is joining me today at the station, and Teddy's got another who came yesterday. I'm not starting for ten days yet."   *53,620*

Dorothy found that she was rather disappointed that her indictment against Evelyn also had broken down in this particular instance, but that did not affect her general untrustworthiness.

"What fun you'll have!" she said. "And I believe your mother did tell me that you would have friends with you. Ah, lunch at last! Thank you, Jacobs."

A glue of beet-root resembling coagulated blood began the repast.

"Mrs. Cook's remembered that I told her you were going to the dentist," said Dorothy enthusiastically, "so she's given us soft food. You're such a favourite of hers: so excited to know you were coming to lunch. Oh, and the dentist. I did ask, didn't I? but then we rambled on to something else."

"I've got to go back at three," said Harry, "and have a whopper out with gas. He couldn't get the gas-man this morning."

"My dear, how brave you are about it," cried Dorothy. "I should be dithering, and you're so cheerful and talkative! I had gas once, and thought I was suffocating in a pit full of green rabbits."

"That's something cheerful for me to look forward to," said Harry.

Dorothy blamed herself for having said this, especially since Harry had told the truth about his tickets. It was not tactful, and if there was one quality on which she might justly pride herself, that was tact. She hastened to remedy her lapse.

"But I was such an unusual case," she said. "My dentist was most interested. He said he had never come across anyone like me before when I told him what I had felt. Almost everybody, he said, positively enjoys gas. They feel as if they were floating in the air among beautiful clouds and hearing heavenly music. Just before you came today, there was a delicious barrel-organ in the Square, with a pet of a monkey to whom I gave some walnuts, playing Tosti's 'Mattinata,' and such a charming organ-grinder: we talked Italian together. Ah, some minced mutton. Mrs. Cook minces mutton so wonderfully; quite a *cordon bleu* at it. Put down the caramel pudding on the table, please, Jacobs, and we'll help ourselves, and I'll ring for the coffee. I think you'd better not go up to see Auntie Alice, Harry. It would tire her to exert herself and talk to you, and at her age she must husband her strength."

"Excuse me, miss," said Jacobs, "but Mrs. Troubridge told me to say she would like to see Mr. Harry after his lunch, if he would come up and have his coffee and cigarette in her bedroom."

"How did she know Mr. Harry was here?" asked Dorothy sharply.

"I told her, miss, when I took up her lunch," said Jacobs. "Just a bit of news."

Dorothy thought it was odd of Auntie Alice to have wished to be left alone before lunch, in case she felt inclined for a nap: surely the more usual time for a nap was after lunch. And it was amazing that she should have asked Harry to have his coffee and a *cigarette* in her bedroom. Auntie Alice disliked the smell of tobacco, so she always said, and in those visits which Dorothy had paid her every day after breakfast, never once had she been asked to indulge herself. Evidently Auntie did not really mind the smell if she wanted to get hold of somebody: a sort of bribe in fact. So, after the caramel pudding, Dorothy had her coffee in the drawing-room while Harry climbed up to the higher storey for his. Anyhow Auntie Alice could not possibly be having a nap now, whether or no she had had one before lunch, and Dorothy had no scruples about playing the piano. She ran through a few scales and exercises, and finding her fingers very lissom, she played Auntie Alice's favourite Polonaise by Chopin; she would enjoy that. Dorothy had heard Carreno play it, and surely there was something of that feminine tenderness combined with masculine strength in her own rendering. She paused at the end: perhaps Auntie Alice and Harry would thump on the floor in applause. Instead she heard the sound of her aunt's shrill, neighing laughter, and Harry joined in with that series of bass cracking noises which betokened merriment. She found the combination of sounds disagreeable: they ought not to laugh together.

Dorothy knew that she had not wanted Harry to see Auntie Alice alone: they might talk, she vaguely felt, about the visit she had proposed and then declined. She wondered now what they were laughing at: perhaps (a pleasant thought but transitory) from sheer joy at hearing that favourite Polonaise. Auntie had not been very bright this morning, and Harry at lunch had really been far from gay—men were such cowards about little afflictions while women bore terrible experiences like childbirth so calmly—but they both seemed to have recovered their spirits. Then, out of nowhere, came the suspicion that they were laughing at something concerning herself. That was probably why Auntie Alice had not asked her to come up too. Or possibly Harry was telling her that amusing riddle about the man sitting down on the spur of the moment. She hoped he would have the honesty to say who had told him. Once more she sat down to her piano, and played that Chopin Prelude in C Minor which always made Auntie Alice feel so melancholy. But at the end came that neighing noise again, shriller than ever.

She looked at the clock: it was a quarter to three already, and Harry was to have a tooth out at three. She must remind him, and ran upstairs. Outside Auntie Alice's door was the vase of mimosa which had gone up with her lunch. So she preferred the smell of tobacco to that sunny fragrance.

Just as she arrived opposite the door, it opened. "Good-bye, darling," said Harry's voice. "She is too priceless for anything, isn't she? Hullo, Dolly!"

"My dear, I was just coming up to tell you that it's getting on for three," she said, "and we must start on your doleful little business. Of course, I'm coming with you. Those dismal minutes in the waiting-room with obsolete copies of *Punch*. No, not a word. Ah, there's Jacobs. Whistle for a hansom, please, Jacobs. Oh, and another riddle: Why did the boy *stand* on the burning deck? Because it was too hot to sit down. Don't you love that? Remember to tell it your mother from me. How she'll cherish it! Now what's your dentist's address?"

"But it's only five minutes' walk from here," said Harry. "Don't whistle for a hansom at all, Jacobs. And don't dream of coming with me, Dolly."

"My dear, I won't be bullied, so that's that! We'll walk there together, and how convenient that your train is at 3.40. I shall drive with you to the station—sometimes people are a little shaky after gas, though they've felt nothing whatever—and pop you into it. Then back here, and a lovely, lovely walk with Strong Mannie after tea. It couldn't work out better: just like a schedule arranged on purpose to suit the Princess of Wales."

"But my friend Jackie Thomas will meet me at the station," said the reluctant Harry. "We're going down together. And please don't bother about me, though it's awfully kind of you. Go out with—with Strong Mannie now."

Dorothy's only answer to this expostulation was to put on her hat. Her presence, she felt sure, would distract his thoughts, and she would have the satisfaction of knowing that he was really going back to his mother's house afterwards. She chattered with-

out pause in the dentist's waiting-room,
noticing a very attractive-looking man on
the opposite side of the magazine-sown
table. He looked in pain, she thought, but as
she rattled on she could not but observe that
his face grew far more cheerful, and when
she asked Harry yet another riddle, he gave
the most delightful smile; evidently she had
made him forget his aching tooth for the moment. She accompanied Harry to the very
door of the operating chamber, and then it
was only natural to talk to this agreeable
stranger, for his smile had broken the ice,
so to speak, and it would be ridiculously con-
ventional if having talked all the time, she
suddenly became mute. She told him that
Harry was her nephew who had come up
from Hampshire that morning—did he
know the New Forest?—owing to this terrible toothache. She always talked to neigh-
bours in trains and buses; it seemed unfriendly not to, when fate had thrown them
together, and there was such a lot to be

learnt from everybody. Indeed the stranger had learned a good deal about family affairs, before Harry came out again.

She made him sit down quietly for a few minutes and ran on to them both to take Harry's mind off what he was no longer suffering, till it was time to start for the station. There a large silent young man was waiting for him, whom Dorothy intuitively felt that she did not trust: he did not meet her eye when she asked him a quantity of questions as to whether he was fond of reading and of playing golf, and she charged him not to allow Harry to sit in a draught after having had such a large tooth out. She stood talking to them on the platform through the open window of their carriage, though Harry begged her not to wait. The silent untrustworthy friend soon effaced himself behind the evening paper, but he was visible to Dorothy outside the glass, and he broke into a broad grin when Harry for the third time urged her to go: Strong Mannie would be wanting his walk. She scolded them playfully for travelling first-class; it was a great waste of money, and third-class carriages were just as comfortable and people were so much more sociable. She kissed her hand and sent her fondest love to Evelyn as the train began to move, and the odious friend shut the window smartly. But after all she had told him that Harry must not sit in a draught.

III

Dorothy's expansiveness and volubility both satisfied and stimulated the urge of some frustrated craving. She hurried home, she had an early tea, and put Chang on his lead to take him for his walk in the Park. The lure of this warm spring day which coursed with such effervescence in her veins made languor in his Chinese blood, and he dragged and loitered, and when they came to the Park and he could go free, he did not gallop and gambol heraldically as was his wont, but lagged behind and sat down on the grass and gazed with bulgy eyes at nothing at all. Certainly he was not ill for he had eaten an excellent dinner; and she was hurt to see his selfishness when she had planned to take him a lovely walk round the Serpentine. Dorothy was very fond of that walk, she enjoyed seeing the gulls swoop and circle above the water and looking at so many babies taking the air in their perambulators. But she could not drag Chang all that way and really it was a thankless task to be always contriving pleasure for that selfish little dog. But perhaps Chang was no worse than those members of the human race to whom she devoted herself, beguiling them with bright talk, and cheering their hours of pain and anxiety. How she had given her time and energies to others today: how she had looked after Harry in particular and with what personal service. She never expected from him any expression of gratitude—anyone who had lived so long with Auntie Alice would have quite ceased to look for that—and gratitude after all was not the species of recompense which she desired. What she did miss in him was something more subtle and spontaneous than a mere acknowledgement of favours received; never for a moment had any gleam of responsive gaiety and comradeship answered her brightness, yet when he was having his coffee and cigarette with Auntie Alice there had been peals of merriment from her bedroom. Once again it occurred to her that talk about her had evoked those shrill neighs and cracks, and now she remembered, in parenthesis, as it were, that when he came out he had said, "She is too priceless for anything, isn't she?" Could that have referred to her, and have been the cause of their laughter? But that was one of those random uncontrolled speculations for which there was no real foundation and she continued not to control it. And Sylvia's ribaldry about the weed-killer....

A young man and a woman much older than he with their arms round each other's waists came strolling along the path by the seat where Dorothy was resting for Chang's sake. She was a short dumpy body with a slack, pretty face on which her companion's eyes dwelt with absorbed pleasure, and Dorothy was suddenly and surprisedly aware that she envied her. They sat down on her seat and began to sing, their faces glued together. She rose: really it was too disgusting that people should behave like that: the police ought to stop it, and putting Chang on his lead again, she hauled him away.

Dorothy had the useful accomplishment of dismissing from the sphere of active consciousness all unpleasant impressions. Of course she could not, with her excellent memory, entirely forget them, but she put them away in some dark cupboard in her mind, where she could find them again if she wanted them. She had stowed several away since she had taken Chang out for his early walk this morning, and as she opened the cupboard door to thrust in this last one, she had a glimpse of the others, gleaming like grotesque little lustre mugs on dusty shelves, and every one of them seemed to commemorate some instance of her having been unwanted or slighted or misunderstood. Chang, the piano-tuner, Mrs. Cook, Evelyn, Auntie Alice, Sylvia, the Vicar and Virginia, Harry and his horrid friend had all contributed to the collection. She had tried in one way or another to be helpful or cheering or friendly to each one of them, and no response had she kindled. Indeed of all the people with whom she had had contact today, that stranger in the dentist's waiting-room was the only one from whom she had received any tribute of appreciation. Now there was this horrid couple who had come and sat on her bench while, a few yards farther on, there was another quite untenanted, who must be forgotten too. She pushed them into the cupboard, but the door would not completely close and remained ajar. Indeed it was impossible to shut it, so full were the shelves.

The cool of the day had revitalised Strong Mannie, and now he tugged at his lead instead of lagging: he gambolled round her winding it about her skirts, he darted to left and right, and she released him. Perhaps he understood her better than anyone else: he guessed, did he, that she had intended to give him a lovely walk by the Serpentine. Away he bounded over the tussocky grass, and Dorothy followed after a backward glance at the lascivious couple she had left. The tokens of their intimacy had grown more manifest and they had ceased to sing.

She turned her back on them and on that half-opened cupboard door behind which were ranged so many distasteful mementos, and began to meditate on something of more practical significance. This subject was constantly simmering and bubbling in her mind, like some steaming pool in volcanic soil, and now and then, like an intermittent geyser, it shot up in a hot jet. For five years now—five long self-sacrificing years—ever since her father's death, she had lived with this widowed sister of his. The arrangement originally had been supposed to be temporary. She was her father's only daughter; Bernard, her only brother, had a wife and family of his own, and though Dorothy had suggested that she might make her home with him, Evelyn had been quite positive that it wouldn't do at all. Then Auntie Alice, a lonely widow in want of companionship, had offered to give Dorothy a home for the present, and the temporary arrangement had now assumed the aspect of something permanent. Dorothy had an income of her own of £400 a year, out of which she contributed £150 towards household expenses. It often struck her that this was a very advantageous contract for Auntie Alice. She had not to take a larger house, or increase her staff of servants: Dorothy occupied a spare bedroom, and had a minute sitting-room, really no bigger than a box-room. In return Auntie Alice received this solid contribution to her income, and gained a lively and cheerful companion. Elderly widow ladies often had someone to live with them, to whom they gave a salary as well as board and lodging, but Auntie Alice's companion paid to her annually a sum which must more than cover the expenses of board and lodging (for the house was run on very frugal lines except as regards delicacies for Auntie when she was ill) and received no salary at all. "A paying companion: that's what I am," thought Dorothy, envying the freedom of the black-capped gulls which swooped and hovered over the Serpentine.

The geyser spouted. Once again she envisaged herself living independently in a flat of her own on her £400 a year. Surely she had a duty to herself of self-development as well as those day-long duties to others, which she performed so zealously but which seemed to earn such scanty appreciation. She would take up music seriously (the piano was her own) and practise four or five hours a day and soon make up for those wasted years of thoughtful self-rationing. She would study some epoch of history (her essays at school had always earned high commendation) and write articles on it for erudite quarterlies. Of course she would not desert Auntie Alice altogether; she would look out for a small flat somewhere close to Beaconsfield Square, so that she could constantly drop in to lunch or dine with her, and then she could borrow the key of the garden to give Chang his early morning walk and his last outing at night. The flat would need two servants, a house-parlour-maid and a cook, and once more she began to figure out expenses.

Four hundred a year would certainly be a tight fit, if she was to live comfortably though very simply. Rent; wages; board for

herself and her servants; dress; income-tax
(it was sure to go up with that wicked war
in South Africa); pocket-money; holiday
by the seaside or in the country; margin for
doctors and other unforeseen contingencies.
It would be mere bondage to be always
scraping and saving: she would not be able
to devote a free mind to her artistic devel-
opment, if she had constantly to be thinking
of petty economies. At present her board
and lodging cost her less than half her income: she had £250 a year for dress and
diversions. And another very important consideration had arisen, since last the geyser
spouted. More than once lately Aunt Alice
had dropped a word or two which seemed
to imply that Dorothy would be her heir.
If she left her and set up an establishment,
however humble, of her own, it was quite
possible that Auntie, who had a hard, even
a vindictive side to her nature, might leave
her money elsewhere. She was old now, and
she was not very strong.

The geyser suddenly stopped spouting. As if inspiration had come to her from the sunset sky reflected so serenely in the molten waters of the Serpentine, Dorothy saw that there was nothing for it but to continue to make other lives brighter for her presence at the sacrifice of her own freedom. Where would Auntie get another companion like herself? Supposing she inserted an advertisement in some paper: "Wanted: A cheerful female companion to an elderly lady, always at her beck and call, to contribute £150 a year to household expenses," was it likely that anyone would answer it? And if there was an applicant, she would be shewn the box-room which would be her sitting-room, she would be shewn Auntie and learn what was expected of her. But who except Dorothy herself could convey to her what infinite tact and patience was required and what unwearied abandonment of self?

"Auntie is utterly dependent on me," she thought. "She would be lost without me, lit-

tle though she realises it. Not a servant
would remain with her for a week if I wasn't
there to hearten them up and set them an
example. She told me what difficulty she
used to have about them, and now that she
is old and ailing, she would be worried to
death. It would be cruel of me. . . . Where is
my naughty Chang? Chang! Chang! Ah,
there he is close beside me all the time.
Mummie's Strong Mannie must march
home after this lovely walk. Such pretty
sea-gulls!"

Dorothy bought an evening paper on her
way home to read to Auntie Alice before
dinner: that would save one of the servants
going out to fetch it. She glanced at it before she went upstairs. There were columns
about that terrible murder trial, and once
again, as this morning, she got deeply interested in it. It would be very tiresome to read
all this out with the deliberation of speech
to Auntie Alice who would probably prefer
to read it to herself. Besides the principle of

keeping the mind free from all thoughts of wicked and disgraceful deeds would be openly violated, and Dorothy decided to glance through it before taking the paper upstairs. She had hardly begun when suddenly there came the sound of a man's footstep descending the stairs: it passed quickly through the tiled entrance passage to the front door, and before she could go out to see who it was the visitor had left the house.

Very mysterious: who could it be? Not Auntie's doctor, for he, she remembered, was to have come to see his patient much earlier in the afternoon. Instantly a full-fledged solution, capable of sustained flight, soared up from Dorothy's mind, like a phoenix from the ashes of her self-immolation. What could be more likely than that he was Auntie Alice's solicitor, whom she had sent for in order to make some alteration in her will? What that alteration was might easily be conjectured. She had had a private talk with Harry today (Harry was always a fa-

vourite of hers), he had been permitted to
smoke a cigarette in her bedroom, and he
had come out in very good spirits, as if
he had heard something greatly to his advan-
tage. Collateral circumstances supported
this view: Harry had not said a word of
what he and Auntie Alice had been talking
about. That was partly her own fault: she
ought to have asked him and watched his
face very closely to see if he was telling the
truth. ("I always know if people are telling
the truth," she thought, "by watching their
eyes.") And it seemed certain now that
Harry had tried to avoid her when he
stepped off the omnibus this morning. It
must be allowed that on this particular day
he had other business in London, but Auntie
Alice might easily have written to him to
come to see her, unknown to Dorothy, when
next he was in town. Then there was the
suspicious fact that Auntie had not suggested that she should come up with Harry
after lunch. Clearly she had something to

say to Harry privately. Their laughter? She
rejected the idea that it was merriment
caused by the thought of the dismal disap-
pointment that awaited herself at some future date. But with what a web of intrigue
and secret dealings she was surrounded!

What was to be done? Nothing except to
put these suspicions into the dark cupboard,
and continue being kind and helpful. She
went upstairs with the evening paper, pre-
pared to read the proceedings at the Old
Bailey that day to Auntie Alice if she
wished it, or to talk to her or to play that
intricate Patience with her which Auntie
Alice almost invariably won. It gave her
such childlike pleasure to pile card on card
with a swift but unhurrying hand, while
Dorothy grew flustered and confused, and
missed all her opportunities.

Her Aunt seemed very pleased to see her:
she gave her an unusually cordial welcome.

"And you've brought the evening paper

for me, dear?" she asked. "That is kind. More about the trial?"

"Columns, Auntie," said Dorothy. "I guessed you would like to have it. Shall I read it to you?"

"Let us have a little talk first. What have you been doing with yourself all day? Busy all the time, I expect?"

Dorothy wondered whether her extreme cordiality was the prelude to the disclosure she had imagined so vividly. Auntie Alice was like a doctor, she thought, being very bright and encouraging before he told you that there was something seriously wrong. So she would be bright, too, though this might be her swan-song.

"Indeed, I have been busy today," she said. "Such a rush of jobs that had to be done. I popped in to see Sylvia this morning, and had such a lovely heart to heart talk. I hadn't seen her for so long, and it is so wicked to neglect one's friends, don't you think? Then the Vicar earmarked me to do

the Easter decorations in the church: I must
find time for that somehow, he would be so
disappointed if I didn't undertake it. Then
Harry came to lunch with me—of course you
know that—and I took him to the dentist,
and he insisted on my driving to the station
with him afterwards. There was a large pug-
faced friend waiting for him there, whom I
tried so much to like, but I couldn't. What
is it, Auntie Alice, that makes those strong
first impressions? Something intuitive, I
suppose: with me they are never wrong.
Then I snatched a cup of tea and took
Strong Mannie for a long, long walk by the
Serpentine. How he enjoyed it! Such lovely
spring weather and flocks of gulls, and
crowds of people revelling in the sunshine.
Two of them came and sat down on the seat
where I was resting, though there were lots
of other empty ones, and sang together. Not
a very melodious performance, but there
was the joy of life bubbling up in it, if you
know what I mean: though it's so hard to

describe. And they were evidently so devoted to each other, which always makes one feel happy, doesn't it? Ah, I hope I didn't disturb you when I played the piano after lunch. That brave blind tuner has done his work beautifully; I must recommend him to Sylvia before she gives her next musical party. And did you notice I played your favourite Polonaise? I thought you would like to hear that. And such jolly sounds of laughter coming from your room when you were talking to Harry! You are quite a wizard, Auntie Alice. You made him forget the horrid ordeal in front of him. What a tonic laughter is, isn't it? Such a silly expression to say that you nearly *died* of laughing! I'm sure everybody feels better for laughing, and less like dying. How amusing Harry can be, can't he? I longed to know what jokes you were cracking together."

A look of weariness had come over Auntie Alice's face.

"I can't remember what Harry and I

talked about," she said with a suppressed yawn.

Dorothy had been watching her closely. Her eyes wandered about the room, but never once had she looked her niece in the face.

"Perhaps he told you the riddle I asked him," suggested Dorothy. "How he laughed!"

"No: I don't think there was any riddle," said Aunt Alice, not showing the smallest wish to hear it. "But you have had a busy day, dear, seeing such a lot of people. And I had another gentleman visiting me just now."

The chronic ferment in Dorothy's brain was suddenly stilled. A tense rigidity took possession of it as she waited to hear who this visitor was. But the habit of being bright persisted.

"How gay you're getting, Auntie Alice," she said. "Two gentlemen to see you up in your bedroom separately! I'm not sure that it's proper. Who was it?"

"Doctor Dobbie's partner. Poor Doctor Dobbie has suddenly been laid low with influenza and couldn't come this afternoon, so he sent his partner. He gave me such a good account of myself. The swelling has quite gone down and I can get up tomorrow."

Dorothy surged out of her chair and flung her arms round Aunt Alice.

"My dear, what lovely news!" she cried. "How wicked of you not to tell me at once! I didn't ask you how you were because I know how you hate being questioned, don't you? Oh, Auntie Alice, you've no idea what an anxiety you've been to me! And I do remember hearing a man's step coming downstairs just now. I must telegraph to Evelyn before the office closes, so that she will know you're better before she gets my letter that told her you were so very unwell. And how overjoyed Harry will be!"

Aunt Alice disentangled herself.

"And mind you tell her that you can now pay your visit with quite an easy mind," she said. "Why not go tomorrow, Dolly?"

"You naughty woman!" cried Dorothy. "You speak as if you want to get rid of me. But you won't! I shall mount guard over you, Auntie Alice, for I know your spirit, and you'll be doing much more than is good for you and knocking yourself up again. Not a word more about it, or I shall leave the room. There's Chang scratching at the door: how he follows me everywhere, doesn't he? May I let him in and tell him the good news? Chang understands everything I say to him. He will bark for joy."

It was not till she had left her aunt that Dorothy remembered that there was a practice in the church tonight for the auxiliary choir at half-past seven. It would never do to miss it, for her powerful soprano was a tremendous support to more timorous choristers, and under cover of it the most diffident fluted their loudest. She therefore had a hasty dinner, and set forth on foot—it was only five minutes' brisk walking—with a light cloak thrown over her green blouse.

The evening was warm and windless, the last flames of a crimson sunset glowed in the west, and the houses on the opposite side of the Square were silhouetted against it as if cut out of black cardboard. The lamp-lighter (how Stevenson found romance in common things!) was going his rounds, and bouquets of yellow flame sprang up in his wake. Chang wanted to come, too, but Mummie explained to him that she was coming back and would take him for his evening stroll afterwards. In the garden the daffodils gleamed pale, a waft of the scent of wall-flowers spread itself across the road, and the hot sunshine of the day had unfolded the pink buds of the almond trees. The spring night was beginning to weave its magic spell, and was working in the faces of passers-by. This man was hurrying home, so Dorothy's sympathetic imagination pictured him, to the intimacy of the domestic hearth, where the wife awaited his return, and supper was ready, and afterwards they would have a look at their young baby rosily asleep in the cot beside the bed. She felt no pang of jealousy at the thought of their fruitful blisses, for the spell and its kindly quickening worked on her with some intoxicating sweetness. Single figures, girl or boy, lounged at street-corners to be joined at the appointed rendezvous by their companions, some were questing and scouting for those whom the soft darkness might hold for them, and all were eager for the fulfilment of their own needs, and for those who needed them. She would have liked to linger, but it was the choir practice that needed her just now, and she must not disappoint the Vicar, for he looked on her as a mainstay of the amateurs and made a point of attending these practices, having a sonorous bass voice himself. They often walked back to the Square together afterwards, and she had once told him that he had missed his vocation—though of course she did not really mean that—for what would she not have given to have heard him sing the bass solos in Handel's glorious "Messiah"? She had hoped, but in vain, that he would have made some allusion to Madame Albani.

Dorothy had to hurry: she was late already, but probably they would wait for her arrival. There was a crescent moon in the west: that surely was the Paschal Moon, about which she had challenged the Vicar that morning. She would point it out to him after the practice, and remind him of his promise to tell her more about its control over Easter. When she turned into the avenue of pollarded limes which led to the church, she saw it was already lit up, and the jewelled figures of saints and apostles glowed in the painted windows. Her favourite was that of a young slim Lieutenant St.

Martin on horseback (how like he was to Harry!) cutting his crimson cloak approximately in half with his sword, and giving the rather smaller portion to a sepia beggar in a purple loin-cloth. A disdainful Roman corporal (or thereabouts) held the horse's head, wondering, so Dorothy fancifully imagined, what the regiment was coming to, when its officers behaved like that. But ought not St. Martin, if he was a true Christian, to have given his entire cloak to the beggar, and ridden on in only his yellow shorts and sandals? One should surely give up all one had for the sake of others, money or raiment, or, most precious of all, one's time and thought and energies. Personal service inspired by charity "that suffers long and is loud" was the supreme dedication of oneself.... Before she got to the door of the church she heard the organ melodiously booming and the choir (how thin the trebles sounded) beginning one of the Easter hymns. Apparently they had not waited for

her, though she was only a few minutes late,
so she joined in the hymn as soon as she got
inside the church, and glided up the nave
singing "Alleluia" at the top of her voice.
The organist looked round at this splendid
addition to the volume of voices, and the
Vicar shook out a fresh reef in his bass, she
thought, to adjust the balance. How the
hymn now rang and echoed in the vaulted
roof!

The music was simple and familiar, and
did not require much effort of attention.
Dorothy's thoughts, fired by the vernal
night, drifted away to a book she had lately
been reading about primitive religions and
the rites of the pagan world. There was always a great festival of thanksgiving in the
autumn over the ingathering of the harvest
and the vintage, but greatest of all, and accompanied originally by human sacrifice,
was the spring festival to celebrate the an-
nual resurrection and renewal of life. The
Christian religion, so said this interesting

book, had adopted and hallowed these pagan rites to its own uses: Easter, in fact was the spiritual counterpart of those primeval rejoicings. Phrases and verses from the Song of Solomon mingled themselves with the intoning of the Easter psalms. "For lo, the winter is past, the rain is over and gone: the flowers appear on the earth, the time of the singing of birds is come.... Behold thou art fair, my love, thou art fair. . . . His cheeks are as a bed of spices, as sweet flowers." The thought of Easter set itself to the frenzy of love-song and to the fruitful showers and suns of the vernal season. "Blossom by blossom the spring begins," she said to herself. Then there were the matings of birds and beasts, the bright-eyed prowlings and encounters in the darkness of the soft night, or beneath the white illumination of the Paschal Moon.... That brought her wandering fancy back to the Vicar: and lo, the practice was over and past and he was kneeling to say the prayer that concluded it.

"Amen," she sang, and rose from her knees. She would walk back with him now, and ask him if that crescent was the Paschal Moon. Sitting next her was a friend of Aunt Alice's: Mrs. Simpson had heard that she had been ill and enquired after her, and Dorothy told her in the hushed voice appropriate to sacred edifices that the rheumatic swellings had subsided and that Auntie hoped to be downstairs again tomorrow. Yes, she had had several days in bed, and had been so brave and patient.

Dorothy turned round after issuing this lengthy bulletin, and saw the Vicar disappearing into the vestry. No doubt he had left his hat and coat there, and she sat down to wait for him. The auxiliary choir dispersed, and one of the church-wardens (tenor) came out of the vestry and locked the door. Dorothy in a whisper playfully asked him if he had locked the Vicar up: had he been naughty? No: the Vicar, he gravely told her, had already left the church by the outer door of the vestry which led into the avenue. Evidently then he had seen her talking to Mrs. Simpson and, unwilling to interrupt them, was waiting for her outside. She hurried out, but he was not there: the figure of a man, three quarters of the way down the avenue, diminished by distance and walking fast, looked very much like him. Perhaps he had been wise, she thought, not to have waited for her. People, even the auxiliary choir, were given to ill-natured gossip and they might have noticed how often the Vicar walked home in the dark with Miss Vincent. That must be the reason and it was not disagreeable. Indeed, she did not regret his absence. She felt she could scarcely have attended to a discussion, even with him, on the Paschal Moon, so encompassing, so tingling was this sense of springtime.

It was dark under the trees: only a few faint stars glimmered through the pollarded angled boughs that were bursting into leaf, but up the road between them shone the reddish glare of the lamps in the street beyond and the coloured flares outside the music-hall just opposite. Music-halls, she understood, were very disreputable haunts. Songs which no really pure-minded person could possibly have written were sung there and received with favour, and much worse than that, there was a bar, so Sylvia had told her, where women of the laxest morals flaunted themselves and made eyes at men whom they had never seen before, but whom they desired to see again. Sylvia had been to this very music-hall with Toby, and instead of being shocked, she had been immensely amused. A man, not seeing that she was under Toby's protection, had said good evening to her, and asked her to have a glass of port. That was a very disagreeable thing to have happened to a respectable married woman: Dorothy had told Sylvia that she ought to have called for the police at once. Then there was a marvellous woman in the bar, said

Sylvia, the bravest, the most undefeated woman, Toby maintained, that he had ever come across. A mature siren; she might easily, if she had had any luck, have been the mother of grown-up children. But there she was still competing with girls who in point of age could have been her daughters. She was hardly credible: quite enormous with an out-size in bosoms, on which hung a necklace of out-size pearls. She had an *eau de Nil* blouse and a stout face with eyes that looked positively starving. Toby was deeply touched. He left Sylvia quite alone, and went up and spoke to her, and ordered a bottle of champagne. "My dear," said Sylvia, "he had the greatest difficulty in getting away from her: she couldn't believe that a gentleman who stood champagne didn't mean business; she couldn't believe that he didn't want her. But she enjoyed her champagne."

Memories of this conversation came into Dorothy's mind as she stood facing the coloured flares. There was a coarse streak in Sylvia, she had always thought, but the impression that now remained was that Sylvia didn't understand. Sylvia had thought the mature siren merely farcical. A horrid abandoned woman no doubt, but surely she was intelligible.

Dorothy suddenly longed to go in and see how the festival of Spring was being celebrated in this pagan temple of dance and song. The thought gave her a touch of that same joyous leap of the pulse with which she had watched those two boys, Harry and Teddy, shining with the sea and wrestling on the beach. Even if some lewd man, seeing her promenading in the bar, mistook her for quite a different kind of woman and made eyes at her and asked her to have a glass of port, she supposed she could take care of herself. She would make a bleak face to meet his horrid leer, and she would be very dignified and politely decline. She would not be in the least shocked or indig-

nant with him: she would realise that she
had brought this on herself by going to such
a place. The Vicar had once told her in one
of their lovely talks that in all his parochial
experiences and his dealings with the fallen,
nothing had ever shocked him: you were no
good in the world if you were shocked.
When you came across something truly lam-
entable, as he often did, the desire to make
things better swallowed up every other emotion. Dorothy was faintly aware that the
desire to make music-halls better was not
precisely her reason for entering their genial
portals, but she made no further effort at
self-analysis. Only self-centred people ana-
lysed themselves.

She went to the box-office and took a stall.
The fifth item of the programme was going
on, and some performing dogs were doing
their turn. They were very clever, and
Dorothy wondered if she could teach Strong
Mannie to stand on his head and continue
waving his tail. Then an attractive young

lady with a moderately good soprano voice, sang a song reeking with sentimentality, about her grey-eyed boy whom she expected home from the West Indies. Wealthy suitors in his absence had tried to win her, but, though Grey Eyes was only a common sailor, they hadn't a chance for all their gold and gems. This aroused immense enthusiasm and she sang again. Then followed conjuring-tricks. All these items were very pleasant— Dorothy imagined herself singing Grey Eyes at a "parish social evening" in her far more powerful voice with melting effect— but she was disappointed. She left her seat and followed a gangway which was advertised to lead to the bar.

A very stimulating place, bright and glittering. A long bar ran up the entire length of it, sparkling with glass. There were dazzling chandeliers hanging from the ceiling, there were rich red plush sofas against the walls with marble-topped tables in front of

them. It was full, and Dorothy at once per-
ceived that the rites of the pagan festival
were being duly performed. Women in
sumptuous gowns and flowery hats were pa-
rading about singly, with an aloof but genial
air, casting sidelong glances and holding
their mouths ready to smile if they saw sig-
nals flown. The men seemed more purpose-
ful, they gave straight appraising stares. It
was hot, Dorothy had loosened her cloak,
making the emerald-green blouse more
manifest, and one of these males gave her
a long look, lit a cigarette and passed on.
That was an escape: she thought he was
going to speak to her and perhaps offer her
a drink. Two boys approached: one looked
at her with merry eyes, then nudged the
other, directing his attention, and they
smiled and wheeled round. Then, surely,
here was the mature siren whom Sylvia had
spoken of: the stout face, the pearls, the
ample bosom, the *eau de Nil* blouse, and
above all the starving eyes. She walked with

quick little steps, squeezing and shouldering her way along, and turning eager mendicant looks to right and left: there was no question that this was the bravest and most undefeated of women, with whom Toby had drunk champagne.... Presently, coming towards her, Dorothy caught sight of a man, whom, she was certain, she had seen before not many hours ago. For the moment she could not place him, then in a flash she recognised the attractive stranger she had seen in the dentist's waiting-room who had smiled so pleasantly as he listened to her cheering conversation to Harry, and to whom she had chatted while Harry was being gassed. She met his eye, she saw recognition there and smiled at him.

"How very odd we should meet again so soon," she said, "what a good show, isn't it? I missed the earlier turns; such a pity. Those performing dogs, so clever, and those brilliant conjuring tricks. I could not see how any of them were done, could you? What a lot of practice—" Speech died on her lips. He was looking at her quite blankly: it was as if he did not see her. When she ceased speaking, she appeared to become visible to him again.

"You must be mistaking me for someone else," he said, and turned off.

Dorothy knew she had not mistaken him for anybody else: she knew also that he had recognised her, and the frightful thought flashed into her mind that he had taken her for one of "those women," and had no use for her. She hurried from the bar, and went straight out into the street burning with un-merited shame. Then an even more humili-ating explanation of his insolent abruptness supplanted the other. All he thought about was to show her unmistakably that he merely wanted to get rid of her, and to hear no more of her bright chatter. One by one scattered episodes of her busy day recurred to her, and, as she ran over them, all seemed to present themselves as riddles to which there was the same obvious answer.

As she put the latch-key into the lock of her aunt's house, she heard the wheezy bark of Strong Mannie inside. She pressed him close to her, covering him with caresses and speaking to him in that baby language which she was sure he understood. He wanted her, she told him; he had been waiting desolately until Mummie returned to take him for his evening walk. Strong Mannie struggled to get free, but still she held him, and then her eye fell on a parcel directed to her standing on the table in the entrance passage. She put Chang down, and with eager fingers she unwrapped it. It was the jade bowl with love from Sylvia and Toby.

The telephone stood on the table, and she rang up their house. Mr. Atchison was out, said the voice of the stupid footman who did not understand the lift, but he would put her through to Mrs. Atchison. As she waited,

Dorothy wondered how it was that Toby had gone out without Sylvia. Had Sylvia not been quite frank with her that morning? Was there trouble between them after all? ... "Oh, is it you, Dolly?" said Sylvia's voice.

"My dear, I've only this moment come in from such a long choir-practice," said Dorothy, "and there it was waiting for me. How can I thank you and Toby? I don't know what I've done to deserve it. Darling, I feel I oughtn't to take it: it's much too good for me, but, oh, what a joy! And with your love and his; that makes it ever so much more precious. It's even more perfect and lovely than I thought when I just glanced at it this morning, so beautifully carved, and such a pure pale green, like *eau de Nil.* I can't believe it's mine. I shall take it up to bed with me and put it under my pillow, so that if I wake up in the night I shall know it's not a dream. I shall try to come round tomorrow and thank you in person, if you would be in about—" There was a click. Sylvia must have rung off.

Dorothy listened for a moment more, and then put back the receiver. The cord swept the jade bowl from the table, and it crashed into fragments on the tiled floor.

(¹)